MONKEY went for a walk one ~~day~~ and ~~me~~t some friends along the ~~way~~.

MONKEY said,
"How are you?" when he met the . . .

. . . KANGAROO.

MONKEY said, "Hello" to ant and his best friend . . .

. . . ELEPHANT.

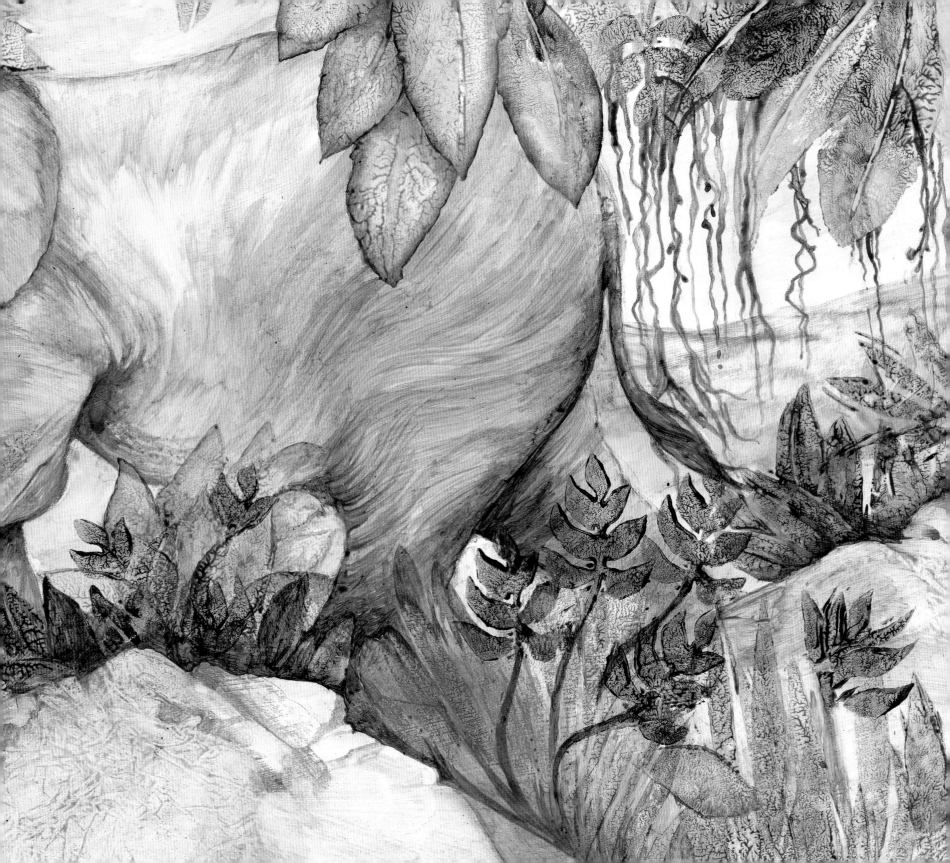

MONKEY said, "Give me a smile!" when he saw the . . .

. . . CROCODILE.

MONKEY saw the branches shake and knew
he'd meet his old friend . . .

. . . SNAKE.

MONKEY said, "This is fun!" and
tried to spot the . . .

. . . CHAMELEON.

MONKEY said,
    "Look out there!" when he saw the . . .

. . . BABY BEAR.

When **MONKEY** reached
the very end of greeting
each and every friend,
it was time for him to
go to bed.